For Karen, John, Whitney,
and Logan Dodson — DD

To the wonderful writers and friends
from Wildacres Writers Workshop!
                                    — MTJ

Mrs. Jeepers
on Vampire Island

There are more books about the Bailey School Kids!
Have you read these adventures?

Mrs. Jeepers on Vampire Island

by Debbie Dadey
and
Marcia Thornton Jones

illustrated by John Steven Gurney

A
LITTLE APPLE
PAPERBACK

SCHOLASTIC INC.
New York   Toronto   London   Auckland   Sydney
Mexico City   New Delhi   Hong Kong   Buenos Aires

Activity illustrations by Heather Saunders.

ISBN 0-439-30641-8

12 11 10 9 8 7 6 5 4 3 2 1   1 2 3 4 5 6/0

Printed in the U.S.A.
First Scholastic printing, September 2001

Contents

1

Discovery Island

"No math. No science. No homework!" Eddie said with a grin as he slapped his ball cap down over his red hair and looked out the bus window. "Three whole days on Discovery Island!"

Liza nodded. "This will be the best field trip ever."

The yellow school bus groaned to a stop in front of the Sheldon City boat docks and the third-graders from Bailey School grabbed their backpacks.

"We still have to do math and science," Howie pointed out to his friends, "only now the math and science count."

"Math always *counts*," Melody said with a giggle. Melody and Liza sat right in front of Eddie and Howie.

"Joke all you want," Howie said, "but

we may have to use our math and science skills to save the animals on Discovery Island. We may even have to save our own lives."

"That's just a fib teachers tell kids to make them work harder," Eddie argued.

"No, it's not," Howie told his friends. "I know it for a fact because my dad is one of the scientists who helped design the park." The kids all knew Howie's dad. He was a scientist at the Federal Aeronautics Technology Station, F.A.T.S. for short.

"Dad told me Discovery Island has challenges that kids have to complete. It takes teamwork, leadership, and courage to succeed."

"What kind of challenges?" Melody asked.

"Things like surviving in the woods at night and swinging across raging rivers on a rope," Howie said with a grin.

Liza swallowed hard. "I don't think I can do all that," she said.

Howie patted his bulging backpack.

"Don't worry. I have flashlights, rope, bottled water, and books — everything we could possibly need."

Liza's face turned the color of sand. "Do you mean we could be in real danger?"

"We're always in danger with Mrs. Jeepers as our teacher," Melody complained.

Mrs. Jeepers stood up at the front of the bus. She wore a white jumpsuit with purple polka dots and a huge broad-brimmed hat to block the sunlight. A long cape was thrown over her shoulders. Her gleaming green brooch was pinned in its usual place at her throat. She had just finished rubbing sunscreen on her nose.

"We'd better put on sunscreen, too," a girl named Carey said from across the aisle. She patted her curly blond hair and batted her eyelashes. "The sun can cause wrinkles."

Eddie pointed out the window to the sky. "We won't have to worry about the

sun today. There's nothing but clouds, clouds, and more clouds."

"I don't think Mrs. Jeepers is worried about wrinkles or sunburn," Melody whispered so that Carey couldn't hear. "Mrs. Jeepers can't be touched by the sun because she's a vampire!"

Most of the third-graders at Bailey Elementary School believed their teacher was a vampire. After all, she came from Transylvania, lived in a haunted house, and always wore a magical brooch that made kids behave.

Liza rubbed lotion on her nose and sniffed. "I don't think going to a dangerous island with a vampire teacher is such a good idea."

"There are trained counselors at every challenge," Howie told her. "They wouldn't let anything happen to us."

"We won't ever be alone with Mrs. Jeepers," Melody said as she patted Liza on the back. "The boat captain will be with us the entire way."

"I hope we get a big white yacht like one of those," Eddie said as the kids jumped off the bus. He pointed to a sparkling white yacht with colorful flags flapping on the bow.

The third-graders followed their teacher as she marched down the dock. They walked right by the big yacht Eddie had seen. They passed boat after gleaming boat. Mrs. Jeepers kept walking until they reached the end of the dock where a lone boat bobbed in the choppy water.

The kids came to a dead stop in front of the boat. Howie's eyes opened wide. Liza grabbed Melody's arm. "I have a bad feeling about this voyage," Liza whispered. "A very bad feeling!"

2

Death Ship

The kids stared at the old sailboat. It didn't look like any of the other boats. This one was totally black, except for several sails and the name LUGOSI painted on the boat's side. They were bloodred.

Mrs. Jeepers didn't seem the least bit concerned that their boat looked creepy. In fact, she looked almost happy. She smiled an odd little half-smile. "This vessel will carry us to our destination," she told the class as the boat captain stepped on deck and peered down at the kids.

The captain was dressed entirely in black, including the captain's hat on her black curly hair. The hat shaded her face from the sun. She nodded to Mrs. Jeepers and grinned at the kids. Her smile

didn't look friendly at all. It looked more like a snarl.

"Ahoy, mateys," the captain said. Her voice sounded as rough as sand, and she had an accent that sounded very much like Mrs. Jeepers'. "Welcome aboard my frigate!"

Mrs. Jeepers led the group across a narrow plank to the boat. The kids huddled on the black deck of the *Lugosi*. It looked like a web of at least one thousand ropes was attached to the red sails slapping in the brisk breeze.

"This ship reminds me of a coffin," Eddie said under his breath so nobody else could hear.

Liza whimpered, "It looks like a death ship."

"Or a giant floating bat," Melody said as she pointed to the front of the boat. She was right. The bow curved back toward the center like huge wings.

"I've never seen a boat with wings before," Eddie muttered. "I hope this thing will float."

Eddie's voice was cut short when he felt the cold grip of long skinny fingers on his shoulder. He gulped as he looked up into the captain's black eyes.

"My boat might as well have wings," she told Eddie, "for it flies effortlessly over the water."

"Great," Eddie said. "Then we'll get to Discovery Island fast." Eddie pulled away from the captain's grasp and plopped down on a bench.

Mrs. Jeepers flashed her green eyes in Eddie's direction. "Do not get too comfortable," she told Eddie as she held out an orange life jacket. "Captain Bela has work for you to do."

"This voyage requires all your help," Captain Bela told them. "Stow your supplies in the crew's quarters and slip on your life jackets. We set sail when all hands are on deck."

The kids found the door that led to the forecastle at the bow of the boat. Inside, there were several berths complete with cots, desk, table, and chairs. The berths were barely bigger than closets.

"We don't have to sleep here, do we?" Liza asked as she dumped her stuff on a cot.

Howie shook his head. "This frigate was probably built a century ago. When it sailed, it was the home to a crew of sailors."

"Is this where the captain stays?" Melody asked.

Howie was digging through his backpack. "The captain's quarters are aft — in the back of the ship," he answered.

"I bet the captain's quarters are bigger," Eddie said as he kicked his pack under a table.

"There's lots more space on deck," Melody said as she pushed her way past her friends. "That's where I'm heading."

As soon as all the kids were back, the

Lugosi pushed off from the dock. It wasn't long before they left the safety of the harbor. The open waters were choppy with foamy waves, and the boat rocked with each one. The red sails flapped overhead and the ropes groaned and creaked in the ocean breeze. Water lapped at the boat's sides and sea spray showered the kids from head to toe.

"What a mess," Melody moaned as she squeezed water from one of her braids.

Liza wiped foam from her face while Howie tucked a book into his pocket.

Eddie stomped in a puddle, splashing more water over them all. "This is not my idea of a boat ride," Eddie griped. "We might as well swim to Discovery Island. We couldn't be any wetter."

No sooner were the words out of his mouth than Captain Bela appeared carrying several mops. "Start swabbing these decks," she ordered, shoving a mop into Eddie's arms.

Before Eddie could complain, Captain

Bela leaned so close her nose almost touched his. "Dry the decks," she ordered. "I wouldn't want you to slip on a puddle and fall overboard. You could be lost at sea — forever!"

3

Vampire Friend

"I hope this choppy water stops soon," Howie said as the kids mopped water.

Liza leaned on her mop and held her stomach. "You're not the only one," she told Howie. "My stomach feels like it's riding a Ferris wheel going three hundred miles an hour."

"I hope the water calms down, too," Eddie said as he threw his mop to the deck. "What kind of field trip makes you do housework?"

But the kids were out of luck. The farther from land they sailed, the choppier the water became. Waves crashed against the sides of the boat. Wind lashed at the sails.

"Why do you keep looking up at the sky?" Melody asked Howie.

Howie pointed to the thick clouds. "I don't like the looks of those," he said.

Eddie shrugged. "They're only clouds. The sky is always full of clouds."

"Not like those," Howie said. He pulled a book out of his pocket and quickly found a picture of different kinds of clouds. "The clouds we're used to seeing are light and wispy," he said. "They're called cirrus clouds. But these are thick and tall. They're called cumulonimbus clouds."

"Thank you, Mr. Weatherman," Eddie said as he rolled his eyes. "Now I know more than I ever wanted to know about something that doesn't matter one bit."

Howie shook his head. "You're wrong, Eddie. Knowing what kind of clouds we're sailing under *does* matter."

"Why?" Liza asked.

"Because cumulonimbus clouds are the worst kind," Howie said. "They mean storms are coming. Bad storms. Storms with lightning, hail — even tornadoes."

"Tornadoes?" Melody said with a gulp.

Howie nodded. "That's not all. With storms, there is wind. Wind makes waves even rougher."

Liza looked absolutely green. So did most of the kids as the boat bounced higher and higher on the waves.

The only person who seemed happy was Captain Bela. In fact, she seemed to really enjoy the salty water. She grinned and licked the salt water that splattered her face.

"Yuck," Melody said. "Doesn't she know you can't drink salt water?"

Howie dropped his mop on the deck and pulled his friends away from Captain Bela. "I think we may have a problem."

"Right," Melody said. "The clouds. You already told us."

"Besides the clouds," Howie said. He nodded in Captain Bela's direction. "There is one other liquid on Earth that resembles seawater," he told them. "Blood."

Melody gulped. Liza shivered. Eddie's eyes got big. "Do you mean Captain Bela may be one of Mrs. Jeepers' vampire friends?" Eddie asked.

"That would explain how Mrs. Jeepers found out about this boat," Melody pointed out.

They looked at Captain Bela. She grinned back at the kids as if she were eyeing her dinner.

Liza held her stomach. "I hope we get to Discovery Island fast."

"I hope we do, too," Howie told her in a worried voice as he pointed to the clouds in the sky. "If we don't, we may be in big trouble. Storm trouble."

4

The Not-So-Perfect Storm

"We're going to die!" Liza screamed as a huge bolt of lightning streaked through the sky. Thunder rumbled. Wind howled around the *Lugosi*. Waves splashed over the sides of the boat. Every other third-grader screamed and ran belowdecks to the captain's quarters — except for Liza, Melody, Howie, and Eddie. Even Mrs. Jeepers and Captain Bela disappeared down below.

Melody grabbed Liza and pulled her close to the *Lugosi*'s aft door. Their mops slid across the deck into the dark waves. Rain pelted the girls.

"Awesome," Eddie said as another bolt of lightning tore through the sky. The thunder was so loud the kids had to

22

cover their ears. "I bet this is the storm of the century."

Howie yelled at Eddie. "We'd better get below. This is dangerous."

"That's why I like it," Eddie said. A huge wave crashed across the boat, throwing Eddie and Howie onto the deck.

Eddie hopped up on the slippery deck, his face covered with sea foam. Liza held on to the outside cabin wall and giggled. "Eddie, you look like a sea monkey."

"He's going to be a drowned sea monkey if we don't get inside," Melody shouted over the pounding rain.

"Let's go!" Howie shouted. The four kids grabbed the cabin door handle at the same time and pulled. Nothing happened.

"It's stuck!" Eddie yelled.

Liza started crying. "They've locked us out. We're going to die!"

Melody pounded on the door. "They must not realize we're still out here. Help!" she screamed.

"Brace yourself," Howie hollered. "Here comes another wave."

The kids looked over their shoulders. A huge black wall of water headed straight for them. "Hold on!" Eddie screamed.

The water hit them like a blast from a water cannon. The kids slammed into the door faces first, but they held on to the door handle as the water washed off the deck.

"We're locked out!" Melody screamed.

"Quick. To the front of the boat!" Howie yelled. The kids clung to the ropes and pulled themselves across the slippery deck. They braced themselves every time a wave washed over the sides. Finally they reached the bow of the boat.

The kids yanked open the heavy door to the forecastle berths and slammed it shut just as another wall of water crashed against the cabin. The whole boat shuddered. "It's the end!" Liza screamed.

5

Off Course

Liza opened her eyes. "Are we dead yet?" she asked when it was quiet enough for her friends to hear. It seemed like they had been huddled inside the *Lugosi*'s forecastle for hours.

Melody shook her head. "The storm must be over," she said.

"There's one way to find out," Eddie said, grabbing the cabin door handle.

"Wait," Liza said, stopping Eddie. "Another blast of water could be right outside the door."

Howie shook his head. "Listen." The kids stood in silence. No wind. No rain.

"I don't hear a thing," Eddie said. "It must be safe."

Howie gulped and whispered, "Unless we're in the eye of a hurricane."

"Do you mean a storm can see us?" Lisa asked.

Howie blocked their way. "The eye is the center of a hurricane," he explained. "If this is the eye, that would mean we've only made it through half of the storm."

Eddie pushed past Howie and pulled open the door. The sun was edging its way around a cloud.

"Thank goodness we made it," Liza said. "And it wasn't a hurricane."

"Don't be so sure," Melody said as they made their way to the back of the boat. "Look at the sails." The huge bloodred sails hung in tatters.

"Can we get to Discovery Island without sails?" Liza asked.

"Don't worry," Howie reassured her. "Boats like these always have a backup engine."

Captain Bela threw open the cabin door and came above deck with Mrs. Jeepers in time to hear Howie. Mrs. Jeepers and Captain Bela both shaded their

eyes with their hands to look up at the ruined sail. "I do have a backup engine," Captain Bela told the kids.

Howie nodded. "See, I told you."

"Unfortunately," Captain Bela continued, "the storm shattered the engine along with the mainsail. We were blown off course as well."

Mrs. Jeepers touched the green brooch she always wore at her neck. "You mean, you do not know where we are?"

Captain Bela hung her head so only her black cap showed. "I am afraid I have no idea. The storm knocked out the radios, too."

Howie pushed to the front. "Isn't this ship guided by satellites?"

Captain Bela sighed and shook her head. "Only new ships have that power. I must rely on older instruments to guide my boat. Unfortunately, my chronometer and sextant were crushed during the storm."

As soon as Carey heard the bad news

she started crying. Several other third-graders came on deck and cried, too. In a few minutes the whole class would be sobbing.

"Crying won't solve anything," Howie said. He raced to the bow and returned with his backpack.

"How can you think about homework at a time like this?" Eddie said with a frown.

"This isn't my homework," Howie told him. "It's my survival pack." Howie pulled out a pair of binoculars from his backpack and looked out over the water. All Eddie could see were long stretches of water, but Howie shouted, "Land ho!"

Captain Bela borrowed Howie's binoculars and looked. A tiny spot of land rose high above the ocean's surface. "He's right!" Captain Bela said. "There is a small island dead ahead. It is time to abandon ship!"

6

Castaways

"I can't swim that far," Liza whimpered.

"Don't worry," Mrs. Jeepers said. "The *Lugosi* is equipped with life rafts." Mrs. Jeepers glanced at Captain Bela.

"Of course," Captain Bela said. "Follow me."

By the time the life rafts were inflated the *Lugosi* had drifted close to the island. Eddie, Melody, Howie, and Liza dropped a small raft overboard and climbed in.

"I am so hungry I could eat this raft," Eddie complained.

"Don't even think about it," Liza said. Her face was as white as sea foam and she held on tight to the sides of the rubber raft. Waves gently bumped the sides.

"Let's get to this island quickly and find some grub," Eddie said. "I hope there's a Burger Doodle there." He grabbed an oar and started rowing.

Unfortunately, Eddie's rowing only made their raft turn in circles. "We have to work together," Melody told Eddie. "Row when I say stroke."

"Stroke! Stroke!" Together Melody and Eddie rowed until their arms felt like spaghetti, then Howie and Liza took over. All around them the other rafts got closer and closer to the island.

"That island doesn't look very friendly," Liza said softly. The kids stared at the sandy shores. Just a short way from the beach a thick dark forest gathered at the base of high craggy cliffs.

Tiny birds darted among the branches, scooping up insects in the air. A few swooped down close to the kids.

"Those don't look like Tweety Birds to me," Liza said.

"They aren't birds," Howie told her. "They're bats."

"Then Mrs. Jeepers should feel right at home," Eddie said.

The four kids looked at Mrs. Jeepers and Captain Bela, who were watching the bats swoop lower and lower.

Liza held her hands to her throat. "Being stranded on a batty island with a vampire teacher isn't my idea of a good time," she said.

"Don't worry," Melody said. "I'm sure the Coast Guard is already looking for us."

"What about that TV show where the characters were stranded on a deserted island?" Liza whimpered. "It was supposed to be a three-hour trip and they ended up stranded for years."

"That's a great show," Eddie said. "I watch the reruns every afternoon."

Howie nodded. "Those castaways were never rescued. They survived by using their wits and working together."

"Are you sure?" Melody said. "I thought they got rescued on a TV special."

Eddie splashed salt water in Melody's face. "It doesn't matter. This isn't a TV special. This is real life."

"I don't want to be stranded forever," Liza whimpered as the rafts bumped onto the shore.

"Don't worry," Melody said. "We'll be fine."

Mrs. Jeepers gathered the students on the beach. She touched her brooch as she surveyed their surroundings.

"I'm cold," Carey whined as she rubbed the goose bumps on her arms.

Mrs. Jeepers helped Captain Bela drag a plastic box onto the beach. Captain Bela opened the box and handed Carey a shiny piece of cloth that looked like aluminum foil. "These are emergency blankets," she told the students. "They will keep us warm until help arrives."

"Until then, we must build a fire for warmth," Mrs. Jeepers said. "Driftwood will make a strong fire. Everyone look for firewood, but make sure to remain on the beach. Stay with your raft buddies. It will be dark soon. We do not want anyone getting lost."

Each group took off their orange life jackets before kicking through thick sand to look for bits of driftwood. Howie wasted no time digging into his backpack and pulling out a small round tool.

"What's that?" Eddie asked.

"It's a compass," Howie explained. "We can use it to help find our way around the island."

"How is that little toy going to help us?" Eddie asked.

"This compass is no toy. It's a tool that always points north. We can search for help," Howie told him, "without worrying about getting lost."

Liza held up her hand. "Wait just a minute. We're not searching for anything except firewood. Mrs. Jeepers told us to stay right here on the beach."

"Mrs. Jeepers doesn't know we have a compass," Howie said. "It's our only hope to find help and get off this island. Do you want to be trapped here forever?"

Liza shook her head, but Melody put her hands on her hips. "We should stay here until the Coast Guard finds us."

"That could be days," Howie said. "Do you really want to stay here without food or water? Do you really want to be stranded on a batty island with Mrs. Jeepers and her vampire buddy?"

Liza gulped, but Eddie pushed into the trees. "Let's go!" he shouted. "I'm starving. We have to find food! This way to Burger Doodle."

"I have a very bad feeling about this," Melody said. "Are you sure you know how to work that compass?"

Howie nodded and patted his backpack. "Don't worry. I have everything we need right here." Liza and Melody took a deep breath and went after the boys. They found a steep trail that led up the side of the cliff. Lush green trees and vines hung all around the kids. The rustling and squawking of birds from overhead followed them.

Melody glanced at the branches. "I feel like someone — or something — is watching our every move," she whispered.

Liza sniffed. "Do you think it could be

Captain Bela leading a flock of vampire bats?"

Eddie used Howie's binoculars to scan the trees. "I'm pretty sure these are just innocent birds and animals," Eddie said, but he didn't sound very sure.

"I hope the creatures in this forest aren't as hungry as we are," Liza said.

"I think we'd better head back before we get lost or eaten by wild animals," Melody told her friends.

"Maybe you're right," Howie said.

"Wait!" Eddie shouted. "Look up there!" Without waiting for his friends, Eddie started climbing up the steep trail to the top of the cliff. His friends had no choice but to follow.

7

Haunted Hotel

"What is it?" Liza panted.

The kids finally reached the top of the cliff. In the clearing before them stood a building.

"It's just an old hotel," Eddie grumbled. "I was hoping it was a Burger Doodle."

The three-story building was definitely old. A rotted porch circled the building, and cobwebs filled every corner. All the windows were dark, and tattered curtains billowed in the breeze. A lopsided sign creaked in the wind. Faded letters read MIDNIGHT INN.

"I don't think anyone has been near this hotel for centuries," Melody said.

"That means this really is a deserted island," Liza said, "and we're stranded."

The kids slowly walked around the en-

tire building. "This must have been a beautiful resort once upon a time," Howie said.

"Once upon a time only happens in fairy tales," Eddie said. "This place is nothing but a run-down dump."

"We should at least take a look inside," Howie pointed out.

"I don't think going inside an abandoned building is such a good idea," Liza said. "We could fall through rotten flooring. The steps could collapse. Rats might live inside. Or," she added with a shiver, "it could be crowded with bats. Vampire bats."

"Maybe we don't have to worry about that," Eddie said. Eddie pointed to an upstairs window. "I think I saw someone up there," he told his friends. "This place may not be abandoned after all!"

"Listen," Howie said.

"I don't hear a thing," Eddie said.

"Exactly," Howie said. "No birds

singing or bugs buzzing. It's as if they won't even get near Midnight Inn."

"Don't be silly," Melody said. "Why wouldn't animals go near a building?"

"There's only one thing that would keep birds and bugs away," Howie said in a whisper. "Fear."

Liza jumped when the front door of Midnight Inn creaked open. A tall, pale woman dressed entirely in black peered

out from the shadows of the old hotel. "Welcome to Midnight Inn," the woman said with a smile. "I have been expecting you. Do come in."

Liza took a step back. "I don't like the looks of this," she whispered to her friends.

"Me neither," Melody whispered back. "She looks like a witch."

"Or a vampire," Liza added.

"Maybe we should get out of here," Howie said.

"I'm with you," Eddie said.

The four kids turned to run. They didn't get far.

8

Midnight Inn

"Ahhh!" Melody screamed as she ran smack-dab into Mrs. Jeepers. Eddie fell to the ground with a thud after slamming into Captain Bela. Liza grabbed Howie and shivered.

Mrs. Jeepers' green eyes flashed in their direction. One green fingernail reached for the brooch at her throat. "You were told to stay near the beach," she said, her voice barely above a whisper. "We have been searching for you."

"W-w-we're sorry," Liza stammered.

Mrs. Jeepers smiled her odd little half-smile at the woman. "I see you have found my good friend Echo Vargen. I hoped we had landed on Vampire Island."

"V . . . Vampire Island?" Melody asked.

Captain Bela nodded. "But of course.

The island is known for its vampire bats."

Liza looked ready to faint, so Howie held her arm as all the other third-graders trooped past them into Midnight Inn. Only Liza, Howie, Melody, and Eddie remained outside.

"What are we going to do?" Liza whimpered. "We're trapped on an island full of vampires."

Melody nodded. "I wouldn't be surprised if Captain Bela and Mrs. Jeepers got us shipwrecked on this island on purpose."

Echo Vargen poked her head out the door. Her big white eyeteeth gleamed in the afternoon light. "Please come in. I have a special room just for you."

The four kids followed Echo Vargen up a long winding staircase to the attic. She opened a squeaky wooden door to show them a tiny room filled with bunk beds. "You sweeties can rest in here until it's

time for me — I mean for everyone — to eat," Echo Vargen said.

Echo Vargen chuckled and licked her teeth before closing the door. The kids looked around the tiny room. It held four bunk beds and nothing else, not even a chair. Eddie climbed a ladder and plopped himself down on a top bunk.

Liza shrugged. "I guess Eddie has the right idea. We might as well make ourselves comfortable."

"Don't get too comfortable," Eddie said in a strange whisper. "We're not staying."

"What are you talking about?" Melody asked. "Where else are we going to go?"

"I don't care," Eddie said as he scrambled down from his bunk. "Anywhere but here with them." Eddie poked one finger up in the air toward the ceiling. Black shapes hung from the light fixtures.

Liza, Melody, and Howie took one look at the ceiling and screamed, "Bats!"

Eddie dashed for the door. "Let's get out of here!"

The four kids raced down the winding steps and straight out the door of Midnight Inn. They didn't stop until they reached the steep trail. "I can't believe Echo would put us in the same room with a colony of bats," Liza panted.

"She probably didn't know they were there," Howie exclaimed.

"Maybe she did," Melody said. "Maybe those bats are her vampire buddies. She wanted them to bite us to turn us into vampires, too!"

9

Four Tickets to Anywhere But Here

"I can't believe we're on an island full of vampires," Liza whimpered in the dark.

"I can't believe we're hiding out in this jungle when we could be inside eating supper," Eddie complained, swatting away a big tree leaf. The four friends had scrambled down the trail and were hiding behind a row of bushes at the base of the cliff.

"What about those bats?" Melody said. "Do you really want to be a vampire bat's snack?"

"I'm so hungry right now I could *eat* a vampire bat," Eddie grumbled. "All I need is a little ice cream and I'd have bat à la mode."

Melody sighed. "I'm hungry, too, but you don't hear me complaining."

Howie listened to the strange animal and insect sounds all around them. Some of them definitely didn't sound friendly. But that's not all they heard.

ROAR!

"What was that?" Eddie gasped.

ROAR!

Liza trembled. "Do vampires come in the monster variety?" she asked.

Howie gulped and tapped Eddie on the shoulder. "I hope that was your stomach rumbling," he said.

Eddie shook his head. "No, that wasn't my stomach."

"Well, it wasn't mine," Melody said. "Let's get out of here."

The kids held hands in the moonlight and made their way along the base of the cliff. "This is just dandy," Liza said. "Our choices are going inside and facing a colony of vampire bats or staying outside and battling a vampire monster."

"Quick, grab something to protect yourself with," Howie suggested. Liza grabbed a rock, Melody picked up a stick, and Howie swung his backpack in front of him like a shield. Eddie pulled some long grass up and waved it in front of his face.

"What's that," Melody asked, "a vampire vegetable?"

"Maybe it'll take his mind off eating me," Eddie grumbled.

ROAR!

"I need a vacation from school field trips," Melody squealed and walked faster.

"Right," Eddie said, "we need four tickets to anywhere but here."

"Come on," Howie urged. "The trail is this way."

ROAR!

Liza, Melody, and Eddie dropped their weapons and ran in the direction Howie pointed. But they only ran for a minute.

Then they started falling. Down. Down. Down. Down.

Thud. Thud. Thud. Thud.

"Where are we?" Liza asked, brushing the dirt out of her hair.

"I'd say we're in a hole," Eddie said.

"A big hole," Melody added.

ROAR!

"Wherever we are," Howie whispered, "I think the vampire monster is getting closer!"

10

Monster's Lair

Howie shined his flashlight above their heads. "It looks like someone *dug* this hole," he told his friends.

"Who would dig a hole in the ground this deep?" Eddie said. "A hole like this is totally useless."

"Unless you were digging a trap," Melody said slowly.

"Trap?" Liza asked, her voice a squeak. "What kind of trap?"

"A kid trap!" Melody said. "And we've fallen right into it."

"Who would want to trap kids?" Liza asked.

"Judging by the size of this hole, it wasn't some*one*," Eddie said. "It was some*thing*! Something big! Like a monster!"

"Do you mean we're trapped in a vampire monster's lair?" Liza asked with a trembling voice. "The monster is making that roar? We have to find a way out of here before it finds us and eats us alive!"

"Calm down," Howie told her. "We don't know there's a vampire monster."

Eddie nodded and started counting on his fingers. "It could be a sea monster, mud monster, snake monster . . ."

Howie grabbed Eddie's hand and stopped him before he could name any more. "It's none of those because there are no such things as monsters," Howie said. "And that includes vampire monsters."

"Then what made this hole?" Liza asked.

"I'm sure there is a logical explanation," Howie said. "We just need to investigate."

Howie flashed his light all around them. "Look," he said, pointing with the beam of his flashlight. "That may help us answer our vampire question."

Liza, Melody, and Eddie looked where Howie's light glowed. Tucked into the rocky cliff was a wooden door. "Where do you think it leads?" Melody asked.

"There's only one way to find out," Eddie said as he took two giant steps to reach the door. He pulled on the rusty metal handle and the door creaked open.

"Don't go in there," Liza warned. "That could be the vampire's bedroom — or even worse — its kitchen!"

"A vampire monster couldn't fit through this door," Eddie told Liza. "It's too small."

"Maybe it's a small monster," Liza whimpered.

Eddie shook his head. "This door was made for humans and I plan to find out where it leads. You can come with me, or you can stand here and wait for a vampire monster to reach in and suck your blood."

Liza jumped next to Eddie. "Lead the way," she told him. "And make it snappy."

Together, the four kids slipped through the door and found themselves inside the cliff wall. Stone steps had been cut into the rock itself. Howie held out his flashlight. It cut a tiny sliver through the pitch-black.

"I guess we hike up," Melody said and placed her sneaker on the first step. Together they climbed until their legs ached and they were out of breath. "I can't go another step," Liza said, her breath coming in ragged pants. "These steps must go to the very top of the cliff."

"It's only a little farther," Howie said. "I can see the end."

Eddie reached the last step. There he found another wooden door. He pushed on it and the four kids silently made their way into a dark room. It felt damp and cold. Spiderwebs brushed their faces.

"Ew!" Liza squealed. "This is creepy."

"What is this place?" Melody whispered as she swatted at the spiderwebs.

Howie's light swept across the room. It was crammed with crates and boxes. "It looks like the cellar," he said, "to Midnight Inn. The steps in the cliffs must be a secret passageway. I bet those stairs lead up into the kitchen," he said as his flashlight lit up a set of stairs in the opposite corner. A sliver of light shone beneath the door at the top of the steps.

"Why would the door to Midnight Inn's cellar exit into a giant hole in the forest?" Liza asked. "Nobody could get out."

"Not unless you can fly," Melody said slowly, "like a vampire bat."

Liza grabbed Howie's arm. "Melody is right. We can't let Mrs. Jeepers and her batty friends find us. You have to think of a way to save us. Before Mrs. Jeepers and her vampire buddies decide they're ready for a midnight snack."

"Wait!" Howie shouted. "If that's what I think it is, we may be saved!" Howie rushed across the storage room. There, sitting on an old table in the corner, was an odd contraption. "This is the kind of radio that ships use to send emergency messages!"

"Great," Eddie said. "Find the microphone and call for help."

"And hurry," Liza said. "This is definitely an emergency. I have spiderwebs in my ears."

"It's not that easy," Howie said as he examined the machine. "There's no microphone. You have to tap out messages in code. Morse code."

"Oh, no," Melody said. "How are we supposed to know the code?"

Howie grinned. He slipped off his backpack and started digging inside for a book. He flipped through the pages until he found what he was looking for. Then he held the book up for his friends to see.

"That just looks like a page of punctuation marks," Eddie said.

"Not punctuation marks," Howie said. "Code. Each combination of dots and dashes represents a letter. All we have to spell out is the international signal for help. SOS. And that's easy. It's three dots, three dashes, and three dots." Howie bent over the radio and tapped out the message, over and over again.

Howie was busy tapping away when Melody heard something. She grabbed Howie's light and flashed it toward the noise. The kids gasped.

There, clustered in the corner, were at

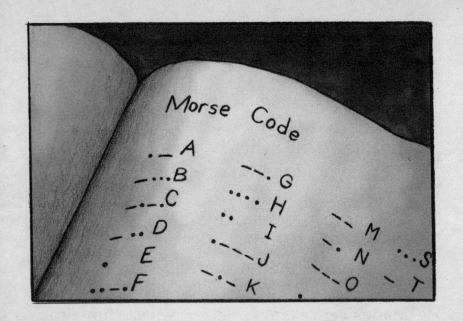

least a hundred bats. Slowly, they turned their heads and peered at the four kids. Then they slowly stretched out their long leathery wings.

Liza gulped. "We'd better get out of here before we become bat breakfast."

"Hurry," Melody said. "Up to the inn."

They were halfway across the cellar when the door at the top of the staircase swung open. They heard the stairs creak-

ing. Someone — or something — was coming toward them.

Now you may choose the ending for
this Bailey School Adventure. Should it
be silly, scary, or scared silly? It's up to
you!

Ending A: Silly

Creak. Creak. Creak.

"Who is it?" Liza asked.

"Or what is it?" Melody said, looking up at the light at the top of the stairs.

Eddie jumped behind Liza and looked over her shoulder. "Whoever it is needs to come on down and act like a man," Eddie snapped.

"Maybe it isn't a man," Howie whispered, clicking off his flashlight. "Maybe it's a vampire."

"Well, this is one vampire that'll be sorry it messed with me," Eddie said, jumping on top of the nearest box. "Come on!" Eddie screamed and karate chopped the air. "I'm ready for you."

Liza pulled on Eddie's leg. "Shhh," she said. "Are you crazy? Get down from there!"

"Hi-yah!" Melody yelled and kicked at the air.

"What are you doing?" Howie asked.

"Unless you have a better idea," Melody said, "you'd better get ready to defend yourself."

Howie shrugged and karate chopped the air. Liza used the dim light from the top of the stairway to search some of the boxes. She pulled out a toilet plunger and held it in front of her.

Melody giggled when she saw Liza jabbing the air with the plunger. "Go, plunger girl," Melody said.

Creak. Creak. Creak.

"Oh, my gosh," Liza squealed. "There it is."

Someone or something appeared on the stairway. It wore the biggest pair of shoes the kids had ever seen. They were green and enormous. "It's a vampire monster!" Melody hissed.

"Hi-yah!" Eddie shouted. "I'll get you, you monster!"

Creak. Creak. Two long legs appeared on the stairway. They wore bright yellow pant legs with green stripes.

"It's a monster that plays golf," Howie snickered.

"This isn't funny," Liza said with a sniff. She felt like she was about to cry.

But Liza didn't cry because the next thing she saw was an enormous round belly and a neon-pink tie. Then a face appeared.

"Ahhhhhh!" Liza screamed. It wasn't a vampire. It wasn't a monster. It wasn't even a werewolf.

"It's a clown!" Eddie shouted, jumping off the box. Sure enough, the man on the steps had a big round red nose, orange hair, and a pointy hat with a pom-pom on top.

"What's a clown doing on Vampire Island?" Howie asked.

"I was just about to ask you kids the same question," the clown said. "What are you kids doing in the cellar at a clown camp?"

"Clown camp?" Melody asked.

"Sure," the clown said. "Echo Vargen runs the best clown school in the country."

"Echo Vargen is a clown?" Liza asked, still holding the plunger.

"Yep," the clown said. "Echo is the best there is."

"I can't believe it," Eddie said.

"My name is Harry Cutter," the clown said. "Come on upstairs and I'll show you the school."

Liza tossed the plunger back in a box and the four kids followed Harry up the creaking steps. Harry opened a cracked wooden door to reveal an explosion of color.

"It's a circus!" Melody squealed.

Harry smiled. "What better place to learn to be a clown?" The kids walked around the large room. Balloons and bright circus pictures lined the walls. Every corner was filled with third-graders and clowns. A popcorn popper and cotton candy machine were churning out treats.

"Let's eat," Eddie squealed. He grabbed a large bag of popcorn and started stuffing his face.

"I can't believe we were stuck in that hole when we could have been in here having fun," Melody snapped, finishing off her bag of popcorn.

"We're here now," Eddie said. "Let's enjoy it."

Eddie, Liza, Melody, and Howie rushed over to a clown car and squeezed in beside Carey and Captain Bela. Howie pushed a button and the car flew apart, sending pink foam balls and kids all over the floor.

Liza giggled and hurried over to a makeup desk. In ten minutes she was transformed into a blue-haired clown.

Howie stood beside a girl named Annie and tried to juggle. "This is easy," Howie bragged, tossing three foam balls into the air. It was a little tougher with wooden clubs, though. Howie ended up bonging himself and Annie on the head. "Ouch!" Howie said.

Melody ran off to watch the clowns standing on their heads and doing handstands. "Awesome," Melody said. "Let me try." Melody stood on her head without any trouble, but when she tried the handstand she fell right onto Echo Vargen. At least Melody thought it was Echo. It was

hard to tell. "I'm sorry," Melody said. "You look very different." Echo Vargen was totally bald, except for two yellow tufts of hair above her big plastic ears. Her clothes were red, white, and blue and covered with spangles and fringe.

Echo nodded. "If you think I'm different, take a look at your teacher." Melody couldn't believe her eyes. Mrs. Jeepers' long red hair stood straight up and her lips were painted bright green. She had on clown clothes and shoes, but she still wore the green brooch at her neck. She never went anywhere without her magical brooch.

Melody giggled at the sight of her teacher in a clown costume, but she laughed out loud when she saw Eddie. "Eddie!" Melody screeched. "You're in your underwear!"

All the third-graders turned to look at Eddie in his underwear. Actually, it was clown underwear — bright lime-green underwear with purple hearts. Eddie wore a red muscleman shirt with fake muscles, a big black handlebar mustache, and huge fake eyebrows.

Eddie flexed a muscle and pulled on a fake flower pinned to his shirt. Water squirted out of the flower and Eddie's underwear fell down.

"AKKK!" Liza screamed, but everyone else laughed because Eddie still had his rolled-up jeans on.

Echo Vargen clapped her hands. "Children, you have been a delight. But now it's time for you to leave. Your rescue boat is here."

Every third-grader groaned. Eddie groaned the loudest.

"Don't worry," Melody told Eddie. "You'll always be the biggest clown at Bailey Elementary School."

Ending B: Scary

The stairs creaked as someone slowly descended toward Melody, Howie, Liza, and Eddie. *Creak. Creak. Creak.*

"Oh, no," Liza squealed. "I bet Echo Vargen is coming to bite us."

Melody gulped. "Along with Mrs. Jeepers and her vampire friend, Captain Bela."

"Turn off your light so they can't see us," Eddie whispered to Howie. Immediately, Howie switched off his small flashlight. The four kids stared up at the dim light coming from the top of the staircase. *Creak. Creak. Creak.* Whatever was up there was definitely coming down.

Liza grabbed Melody's arm and held on tight. Eddie jumped behind Howie.

Liza sniffed. "My nose feels like it's about to bleed." Sometimes when Liza got upset, she had a nosebleed.

"Hold your nose," Howie warned. "If there's one thing we don't need right now, it's blood."

A bloodcurdling squeal came from the steps. Behind the kids, the fluttering of bats turned frantic.

"What was that?" Eddie asked.

"It sounded like a crazy person to me," Liza whispered.

"Bats communicate with high-pitched sonar," Howie said in a whisper.

"I bet Captain Bela just used bat language to say come and get it," Melody said.

Liza gulped. "You mean come and get *us*?"

"We're vampire chow if we don't get out of here," Eddie said.

"Follow me," Howie yelled as he scrambled over boxes and crates. He flung open the back door. His three friends raced after them. Eddie slammed the door shut behind them. They raced back down the steep stairs.

The kids panted from all their running and felt around in the pitch-black. "Great," Melody said as she ran right into a dirt wall. "We're trapped in this hole again with no way out."

ROAR!

"And that vampire monster is still out there. It's heading our way," Liza added with a whimper.

ROAR!

"If I have to choose between one monster and a flock of vampires, I'll take my chances with the monster," Eddie said. He tried jumping up to grab the edge of the hole. There was no way he could reach the top.

"This is the end," Liza said with a whimper. "It was nice knowing you."

"Don't say good-bye just yet," Howie told her as he dug in his backpack. "I have a plan. Eddie and Melody, get down on your knees."

"Begging usually works with my grandmother," Eddie said, "but I don't think it will do any good against hungry vampires."

"I'm not planning on begging," Howie said, pulling rope out of his pack. "I don't have time to explain. If you want to live, do what I say."

Melody and Eddie fell to the ground. Howie kneeled on top of his friends. "I get it," Liza said. "You're making a human pyramid so we can reach the top of the hole. We do that in cheerleading."

Howie nodded and handed her his rope. "Now, it's up to you, Liza. Climb on my back and get out of this hole. Then drop the rope down for us."

"If it doesn't work," Melody said, "thanks for being such a good friend."

"It will work," Liza said. "I promise."

Liza hopped to the top of the human pyramid. When she did, she could easily reach the rim. She pulled herself out of the hole.

"Do you think we'll ever see her again?" Howie asked.

"What if the monster gets her?" Eddie said.

Melody gulped. "Oh, my gosh, what have we done? The vampire monster might be eating Liza right now!"

Howie squinted to see the top of the hole. "Liza will be back," Howie said. He sounded more sure than he felt.

In no time flat the rope was dropped down the hole.

"Hurrah for Liza!" Melody cheered.

The three took turns climbing the rope out of the hole. "Way to go!" Eddie told Liza as they pulled the rope up out of the hole.

ROAR!

"Now, let's get out of here before we have to battle a vampire monster," Liza said.

"Holy Toledo!" Eddie shouted as bats flew toward the kids.

"Run!" Melody screamed. The kids raced away from the bats. They ran into the forest and scrambled through the trees.

"Oh, no," Liza panted. "We're lost. I think we're going in circles."

Howie slapped his forehead. Then he dug his compass and flashlight out of his pocket. "We're not lost anymore," he said. "Follow me to the beach."

"Thank goodness you know about survival skills," Melody told Howie.

Eddie grabbed a vine. "I know about survival skills, too. Watch this!" Eddie swung on the vine and disappeared through the trees.

"Eddie, get back here!" Liza screamed.

Melody put her hands on her hips. "This is no time to play Ape Man." Just then a huge roar came from Eddie's direction.

"Oh, no!" Howie gulped. "The vampire monster has Eddie!"

The kids pushed their way through vines and bushes, making sure to follow the needle of Howie's compass. As they walked, the roaring grew louder and louder.

"I think Howie is leading us straight into the monster's lair," Melody said.

Liza looked ready to cry. "Poor Eddie."

"Poor Eddie my foot," Melody snapped. "There he is."

Eddie hung upside down from a tree. "What took you guys so long?"

Liza started to fuss at Eddie, but a huge roar stopped her.

"Wait," Howie said. The kids stood still and listened. The roaring sound steadily continued. Suddenly, Howie grinned.

"That's no monster," he said, "that's the sound of the waves crashing against the shore! The tide is coming in. If we follow the sound, we'll find our way to the beach!"

Howie was right. Finally, the forest gave way to the sandy beach. The *Lugosi* still bobbed in the shallow water. But the *Lugosi* wasn't alone.

Next to the black boat was a shiny white Coast Guard ship.

"We're saved!" Melody screamed. "They got Howie's SOS signal!"

Eddie slapped Howie on the back. "Remind me never to tease you about being prepared again," Eddie said.

Howie grinned. "Discovery Island will be a breeze compared to this," he said.

Liza gulped. "You don't mean we still have to go there, do you?" she asked.

"Haven't we had enough adventure for one field trip?" Melody asked.

Howie grinned. "Stick with me. Our adventures are just beginning!"

Ending C: Scared Silly

Very slowly, Captain Bela descended the stairs. She wasn't alone. Mrs. Jeepers and Echo Vargen followed right behind her.

Captain Bela slowly reached a bony hand up to switch on a lone lightbulb. A weak light cast long shadows on the cellar wall and on the adults. They were each dressed in a long shiny black cape, with a bloodred lining.

Liza grabbed Melody's arm and whispered, "Welcome to Vampire Island." Even though she was careful to keep her voice low, Echo Vargen heard.

Echo smiled, her white teeth gleaming. "So you know," she said, "about my bats."

Melody gulped. Liza closed her eyes. Howie's lips moved but nothing came out. Eddie wasn't so quiet.

"Of course we know about vampire bats," Eddie said. "Every kid knows the stories."

"Stories?" Captain Bela asked. "You believe they are merely stories?"

Eddie nodded, but he didn't look so sure. "Of course. There are no such things as vampires. Not REAL vampires."

Captain Bela looked at Echo Vargen. Echo Vargen looked at Mrs. Jeepers. Mrs. Jeepers smiled her odd little half-smile. Then she started to laugh. So did Captain Bela and Echo Vargen. They laughed a loud throaty laugh that sent cold chills scampering down all the kids' backs.

"Wh-wh-what's so funny?" Liza stammered.

Echo Vargen stopped laughing and peered down at the kids. "They are not stories," she said slowly. "Vampire bats are real. They are here all around you."

No sooner were the words out of her mouth than the bats clinging to the rafters started to beat their wings. Melody, Liza, Howie, and Eddie looked up to see at least a hundred sets of beady eyes staring right at them.

Melody grasped Liza's hand. "This is the end," Melody said. "You've been a great friend."

Liza nodded. "You, too."

"It's been nice knowing you," Eddie told Howie. "Even if you did drive me crazy with all your books."

"We've had good times," Melody told Eddie.

"And we forgive you for all the times you got us in trouble," Liza added.

"Don't say good-bye yet," Howie said. "I have an idea."

"Then you better do something fast," Melody said under her breath, "before we're bat bait."

Captain Bela and Echo Vargen took another step toward the four kids. When they did, Howie went into action. He jumped over a box, reached for the old radio, and frantically twirled the dials. Suddenly, a high-pitched screech sliced through the air. He turned another dial to make it even louder.

Mrs. Jeepers, Captain Bela, and Echo Vargen grabbed their ears. They turned to flee the sound and bumped into one another, falling into a tangled heap on the ground.

"What are you doing?" Melody screamed.

"No time to explain," Howie said as he grabbed Melody's and Liza's arms and pulled them across the cellar. Eddie followed. They jumped over their teacher, Captain Bela, and Echo Vargen and dashed up the steps to freedom.

"Wake up, everyone!" Howie screamed. "Run for your lives!"

Third-graders poked their heads out of

every room in Midnight Inn. Just then, a hundred bats flew up from the cellar. They flapped around the main floor of Midnight Inn. Kids screamed at the sight. One bat flew into Carey's blond hair. "Help me!" Carey screamed. Howie swatted the bat with his backpack to make it fly away.

"Follow me!" Howie yelled and dashed out the door of Midnight Inn. Without a second thought, every third-grader followed him.

As soon as they reached the night air, Howie pulled his compass and flashlight from his backpack and pointed the way to the beach.

ROAR!

"What's that?!" Liza screamed.

Carey held her hands to her face. "It's a monster!" she shouted. "We're all going to die."

"Not if I can help it," Eddie hollered. "Let's get out of here."

The kids pushed their way through vines and bushes, making sure to follow the needle of Howie's compass.

ROAR!

As they went, the roaring sound grew louder and louder.

"I think Howie is leading us straight into a monster's belly," a kid named Huey said.

"Wait," Howie said. The kids stood still and listened. The roaring steadily continued. Suddenly, Howie grinned.

"That's no monster," he said, "that's the sound of the waves crashing against the cliffs! If we follow the sound, we'll find our way to the beach!"

The kids finally broke through the wall of trees and scrambled onto the beach. The *Lugosi* still bobbed offshore, but the *Lugosi* wasn't alone.

Next to the black boat was a shiny white Coast Guard ship.

"We're saved!" Melody screamed. "They got Howie's SOS!"

Eddie slapped Howie on the back. "Remind me never to tease you about being prepared again," he said.

"How did you know that screeching noise would stop Mrs. Jeepers and her vampire friends?" Liza asked.

Howie pulled another book from his backpack. It was all about animals. "Easy," he told his friends. "According to this, bats find their way using sound. I figured vampires were the same. I just confused their nighttime sonar!"

"Maybe they aren't vampires after all," Eddie said and pointed. Mrs. Jeepers and Captain Bela had just stepped onto the beach. They made their way across the sand to where the Coast Guard boat was moored. Their capes flapped in the sea breeze like giant wings.

"Splendid," Mrs. Jeepers said. "We will make it to Discovery Island this evening after all."

Liza gulped. "You don't mean we still have to go there, do you?" she asked.

"But of course," Mrs. Jeepers said with her odd little half-smile. "After all, our adventures are only beginning!"

Scared Silly
Puzzles
and Activities

Spooky Shipwreck Maze

Melody, Howie, Liza, and
Eddie are lost. Can you
help them find the
path that leads
to the rescue
boat?

Answer on page 117

Mrs. Jeepers' Tropical Cooler

You may need a grown-up to help you with this recipe.

6 cups ginger ale or lemon-lime soda
1 cup maraschino cherry juice*
6 maraschino cherries
2 scoops of cherry ice cream (optional)

1. Pour the soda and cherry juice into a pitcher or large bowl. Stir.

2. For an extra spine-tingling chill, add cherry ice cream to the pitcher and let it melt for a few minutes. Then stir again.

3. Pour this fizzy red brew into six glasses.

4. Add a cherry to each glass for decoration.

5. Toast the tropics with your friends!

*Maraschino cherries are the bright red cherries come packed in a jar.

Castaway Crossword Puzzle

Now that you've read *Mrs. Jeepers on Vampire Island,* do you know the answers to this puzzle?

Across:
1. What did the kids use to swab the decks?
2. Melody thinks Captain Bella's boat looks like what flying creatures?
3. How many days was Mrs. Jeepers' class supposed to spend at Discovery Island?
4. What color did Lisa turn during the storm?

Down:
2. What color is most of the *Lugosi*?
5. After the storm, who was the first person to spot land?
6. What caused the shipwreck?

Answer on page 117

Make Your Own Compass

Lost in the woods? Need to find north? It's easy. When the Bailey School Kids were lost on Vampire Island, Howie used a compass to find the way back to shore. Now you can make your own compass.

You will need:

A magnet
2 sewing needles
A pencil or pen
A short piece of threa
A clear plastic cup

Rub the magnet along the needle from the thick end to the point. Always rub in the same direction. Be patient. You'll have to rub at least 25 times to make the needle act like a magnet. You'll know the needle is magnetized when you can use it to pick up another needle.

Tie one end of the thread to the middle of the needle. Tie the other end of the thread to the middle of a pencil.

Place the plastic cup on a table or other flat surface. Rest the pencil along the top of the cup and let the needle hang. Wait for the needle to stop swinging. The thicker end of the needle will point true north.

Remember: If you are facing true north, east will be to your right and west to your left. South will be behind you.

Batty Word Search

Find the words hidden below. Words can be horizontal, vertical, diagonal, and even backward!

Words: CLOUDS, SAND, COMPASS, VAMPIRE, SHIP, SAILS, ISLAND, DOCK, SWIM, WAVES

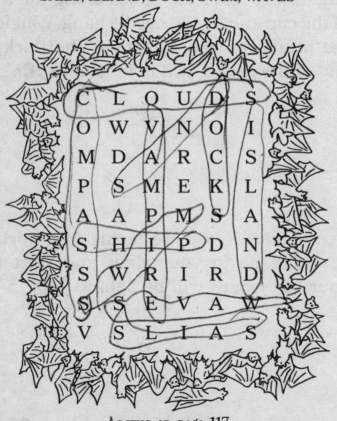

C L O U D S
O W V N O I
M D A R C S
P S M E K L
A A P M S A
S H I P D N
S W R I R D
S S E V A W
V S L I A S

Answer on page 117

Howie's Survival Pack Puzzler

It's time to test your memory. Throughout *Mrs. Jeepers on Vampire Island*, Howie uses items from his backpack to help the Bailey School Kids get out of batty situations. Can you name all the survival gear packed in Howie's backpack? Here's a hint: There are eight items named in the book.

1. _compass_
2. _wether book_
3. _bonoclars_
4. _bottledwater_
5. _rope_
6. _animl book_
7. _mores codebook_
8. _flashlights_

Answer on page 118

Haunted Hotel Fill-ins

On pages 112–113 is a passage taken from *Mrs. Jeepers on Vampire Island*. But, uh-oh — some words are missing! Can you help Mrs. Jeepers' class fill in the blanks?

Before you even look at the passages, fill in the blanks below. Try to pick words that are as silly, funny, or spooky as possible. When you are done, copy the words in order into the story. And get ready to laugh out loud! You'll have your own brand-new BSK adventure!

Your name: _Helen_

Noun: _Cat_

Name of a friend: _Annika_

Same noun as before: _Cat_

Adjective: black

Noun: window

Plural noun: windows

Adjective: spocky

Plural noun: doors

Noun: _____

Time of day: _____

Length of time: _____

Name of a friend: _____

Adjective: _____

Your name: _____

111

"What is it?" (_____)
your name

panted.

"It's just an old (_____),"
noun

(_____) grumbled. "I was
name of friend

hoping it was a Burger Doodle." The

three-story (_____) was
same noun as before

definitely (_____). A rotted
adjective

(_____) circled the building,
noun

and (_____) filled every corner.
plural noun

All the windows were (_____),
adjective

and tattered (_____) billowed
plural noun

in the breeze. A lopsided (_____)
                                 noun

creaked in the wind. Faded letters

said: (_____) INN.
          time of day

   "I don't think anyone has been

near this hotel for (_____),"
                       length of time

(_____) said.
  name of a friend

   "That means this really is a

(_____) island," (_____)
   adjective   your name

said, "and we're stranded!"

113

Fun Tropical Facts

Mrs. Jeeper's on Vampire Island is packed with fun trivia and facts. Check this out!

- **Cirrus clouds** are light and wispy.

- **Cumulonimbus clouds** are thick and tall. They are the most dangerous kinds of clouds. They mean storms are coming — with lightning, hail, and even tornadoes.

- The **eye of a hurricane** is the center of a hurricane. It's calm there.

- The **bow** is the front part of a boat. The **aft** is the back part. And the **forecastle** is the crew's quarters, usually found in the bow of the boat.

- Bats find their way using high-pitched sound. This is called **sonar**.

- **Morse code** uses a series of dots and dashes to send messages. Each combination of dots and dashes represents a letter. The international signal for help is **SOS**. It's just three dots, three dashes, and three dots.

Vampire Tag

Here's a fun game to play
if you are ever lost on a
deserted island. It also
works on the playground,
in the backyard, or in any
wide-open space.

First, choose one person to be the Vampire. The Vampire's job is to chase the other players and try to tag them.

If the Vampire tags another player, that player becomes part of the Vampire. The tagged player has to put her/his hands on the Vampire's shoulders to form a chain. The new, larger Vampire can only move as a chain. Hands cannot be removed from shoulders.

This chain of Vampires chases the rest of the players until they've tagged almost everyone. The last person to escape the Vampire is the winner!

Puzzle Answers

Spooky Shipwreck Maze

Castaway Crossword Puzzle

Batty Word Search

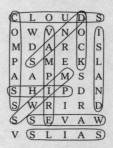

Howie's Survival Pack Puzzler

1. binoculars
2. bottled water
3. flashlight
4. compass
5. rope
6. book on clouds
7. book on Morse code
8. book about animals

Creepy, weird, wacky, and funny things happen to the Bailey School Kids!™ Collect and read them all!

Available wherever you buy books, or use this order form

Scholastic Inc., P.O. Box 7502, Jefferson City, MO 65102

Please send me the books I have checked above. I am enclosing $_____ (please add $2.00 to cover shipping and handling). Send check or money order — no cash or C.O.D.s please.

Name _____

Address _____

City_____ State/Zip _____

Please allow four to six weeks for delivery. Offer good in the U.S. only. Sorry, mail orders are not available to residents of Canada. Prices subject to change.   BSK801